# Saber-Tooth Trap

by Dawn Bentley

Illustrated by Trevor Reaveley

*To my little tiger, Jackson Bentley Harshbarger—I love you!*—D.B.

Book copyright © 2005 Trudy Corporation
and the Smithsonian Institution, Washington DC 20560

Published by Soundprints Division of Trudy Corporation, Norwalk, Connecticut.

Book design: Marcin D. Pilchowski
Book layout: Bettina M. Wilhelm
Editor: Laura Gates Galvin
Illustration studio: Artful Doodlers

First Edition 2005
10 9 8 7 6 5 4 3 2 1
Printed in China

*Acknowledgements:*
   Our very special thanks to Dr. Don E. Wilson of the Department of Systematic Biology at the Smithsonian Institution's National Museum of Natural History.
   Soundprints would also like to thank Ellen Nanney and Katie Mann of the Smithsonian Institution's Office of Product Development and Licensing for their help in the creation of this book.

*Library of Congress Cataloging-in-Publication Data is on file with the publisher and the Library of Congress.*

# SABER-TOOTH TRAP

by Dawn Bentley

Illustrated by Trevor Reaveley

 **Sound**prints
*Where Children Discover...*

It is the Ice Age, but not a bit of snow or ice can be seen. Unlike some other parts of the world, this sunny grassland is warm and humid. Frogs and turtles gather near a stream. Grasshoppers jump, flies buzz, and scorpions scuttle by while Saber-Tooth Tiger rests under a big oak tree.

Saber-Tooth Tiger's ears twitch. He hears something in the distance. He jumps to his feet and listens more closely. It sounds like a pack of howling dire wolves.

Saber-Tooth Tiger opens his mighty jaws and lets out a powerful roar. His two long saber teeth are an awesome sight. Saber-Tooth Tiger depends on his teeth for protection and hunting. But these fierce-looking teeth can be fragile. Saber-Tooth Tiger must be careful not to bite into anything hard. One chomp of a rock or bone could break his precious fangs.

Saber-Tooth Tiger hears the dire wolves again. As he runs toward the sound, he sees other members of his pack headed in the same direction. Together, the saber-tooth cats can hunt down even the largest of beasts.

Saber-Tooth Tiger approaches the lake where the sound is coming from. Although the water looks calm and inviting, it is actually very dangerous. Just under the water's surface is a very sticky tar-like substance. A mastodon is stuck in the tar and can't get out.

The howling wolves are hungry. They try
to reach the mastodon, but the tar is too sticky.
One of the wolves becomes caught in the glue-like
tar. Now two animals are trapped in the tar!
Vultures and hawks circle above, waiting for
the chance to swoop down and feast.

Saber-Tooth Tiger is hungry, too. The wolf and the mastodon look like easy prey. Saber-Tooth Tiger eagerly moves toward the wolf. He puts one paw into the water, and then quickly pulls it out when he feels it sinking into the gooey tar. He is lucky this time—he wasn't trapped.

Saber-Tooth Tiger leaves the lake to look for food somewhere else. In the open grassland, he hears a thundering sound. A herd of bison is running in the distance. What are they running from? Saber-Tooth Tiger moves closer and sees the bison are fleeing from the other saber-tooth cats. He runs to join them.

Saber-Tooth Tiger has short, powerful legs, better suited for pouncing and leaping than for racing. The saber-tooth cats will wait for one of the weaker, slower bison to fall behind, and then use their strong legs and long teeth to bring it down. Saber-Tooth Tiger waits and waits, but the bison stay packed close together. There doesn't seem to be a weak one in the herd!

Then Saber-Tooth Tiger sees something moving near the sagebrush. It's a Harlan ground sloth, eating plants. While the other cats continue to chase the bison, Saber-Tooth Tiger goes after the six-foot, 3,500-pound ground sloth all by himself!

Saber-Tooth Tiger will have to be careful. If he bites into one of the little protective bones under the sloth's skin, he might break one of his huge fangs. Quickly, Saber-Tooth Tiger pounces on the unsuspecting sloth and knocks it to the ground.

The other saber-tooth cats race over to have lunch. It has been a long, tiring afternoon in search of this well-deserved meal. Saber-Tooth Tiger yawns, his dagger-like teeth glinting in the sun. With his belly full, he returns to the shade of the oak tree and falls fast asleep.

# ABOUT THE SABER-TOOTH TIGER

The particular type of saber-tooth tiger in this story is the *Smilodon* species. Named for the two long teeth protruding from its mouth, *Smilodon* (SMY-luh-don) means "knife tooth." The long teeth helped saber-tooth tigers hunt for food. These fangs were very sharp and could easily slice through soft tissue, but saber-tooth tigers had to be careful not to bite into bone or their teeth would break.

We know that saber-tooth tigers were not fast runners because their legs were short and they had short, bobbed tails. Fast-running animals generally have longer tails to help them stay balanced at higher speeds. Saber-tooth tigers had very strong front legs that helped them spring onto prey.

Saber-tooth tigers lived on Earth until about 10,000 years ago. People existed during the time of the saber-tooth tiger. Scientists have found saber-tooth tiger fossils in North America and Europe. They have learned about saber-tooth tigers from these fossils, as well as from frozen, mummified carcasses and ancient cave drawings.

# PICTORIAL GLOSSARY

▲ Saber-Tooth Tiger

▲ Bison

▲ Ground Sloth

▲ Frog

▲ **Dire Wolf**

▲ **Turtle**

▲ **Mastodon**

▲ **Scorpion**